To *Hermine* and *Helen*

from

Jack and *Roger*

The Camel

who took a walk

STORY BY JACK TWORKOV

PICTURES BY ROGER DUVOISIN

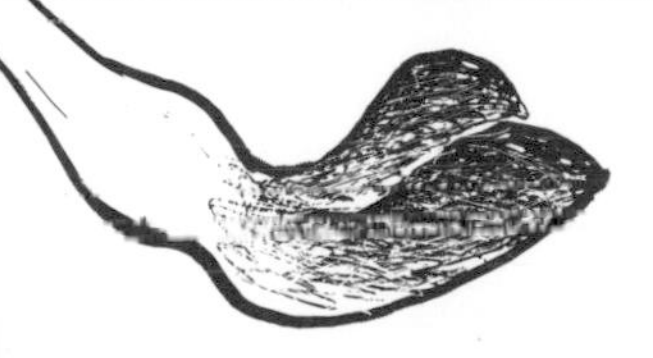

E. P. DUTTON · NEW YORK

Cover adaptation for this edition by Jon Agee

ISBN 0-525-44476-9

Published in the United States by
E. P. Dutton, New York, N.Y.,
a division of Penguin Books USA Inc.

Published simultaneously in Canada by
Fitzhenry & Whiteside Limited, Toronto

Printed in Hong Kong
First Unicorn Edition 1989
10 9 8 7 6 5 4 3 2 1

The forest was dark and very quiet.
Not a creature was stirring.
Even the wind had stopped breathing.
Not a leaf was falling,
not a blade of grass was moving.
And do you know why this was so?
Because
it was just the time between night and day,
when night was ending
and day was about to begin.

Night in the forest is very dark,
and it creeps away slowly.

At the time this story begins
it was still very dark in the forest.
It was also very warm.

All the creatures were very quiet.
But the quietest of all was the tiger.

The tiger was lying
at the foot of a tree by the side of a road
that divided the forest in half.
It would have been very hard
to see the tiger because he was hidden
by leaves, flowers, vines and grasses.
He was hidden also by the darkness.

Suddenly
the first glimmer of light trembled in the sky.
The sky, the forest, and even the air
began to turn blue.

Just then,
on the road that divided the forest in half,
far far up that road —
right near the horizon,
which is where the sky and the ground meet,
something —
yes, something was moving.

Now
the tiger might have been sleeping!
But if you could have looked into his face
you would have seen that one eye,
the eye facing the thing that was moving,
was open just the tiniest, tiniest crack.

And when a tiger's eye
is open the tiniest crack,
then you know that the tiger is *not* sleeping
as he would have you believe. But—
he is watching and thinking.

Now this thing that was moving,
and that the tiger was watching,
was drawing nearer and nearer.
The sky was getting bluer and bluer.
The light on the road had turned pink,
so you could see that the thing was—
you will be surprised

a very beautiful camel.

A very beautiful camel
with soft brown eyes
was just taking her morning walk.
She walked — oh, so slowly, so gracefully,
with her head way up in the air.
Her nose
smelled the early morning sweetness,
and her eyes
took in all the blue and pink colors
of the sky.

And the tiger
who was lying at the foot of the tree
was thinking,
"As soon as this beautiful camel comes
to where the shadow of the tree falls
across the road —
I am going to pounce on her!"

But the tiger was not the only one
who saw the camel
walking down the road.

Way up in the tree,
on a branch directly over the tiger,
sat a little monkey.
And he knew
what the tiger was thinking about!
And so he, very quietly,
reached for a cocoanut
and held it in his hands.
And he said to himself,
"Just as soon as the tiger
is about to pounce on the camel —
I will drop this cocoanut on his head."

And all the while
the beautiful camel walked gracefully
down the road,
turning her pretty head this way and that,
while the sky got brighter and brighter.

But the tiger and the monkey
were not the only ones
who saw the beautiful camel.

On the same tree
a little squirrel with its bright little eyes
had seen what was going on.
And the little squirrel, very quietly,
crept up right behind the monkey's tail.
And the little squirrel said to himself,
"As soon as the monkey is ready
to drop the cocoanut
on the tiger's head — I will *bite* his tail!"

All the while, the beautiful camel
walked gracefully down the road
turning her pretty head this way and that,
while the sky grew brighter and brighter.

But the tiger,
the monkey, and the squirrel
were not the only ones
who saw the beautiful camel.

A little bird was watching
what the tiger, the monkey,
and the squirrel were up to.
And the little bird said to himself,
"Aha! I know what *I* shall do —
As soon as the squirrel is ready
to bite the monkey's tail,
I shall pounce, with my sharp claws,
upon his tiny head."

And now the tiger was so excited —
so excited, he forgot to keep his tail still.
He swished it from side to side,
this way and that way.

Meanwhile,
the camel was getting nearer and nearer,
and the sun was getting hotter and hotter,
and the camel
was getting warmer and warmer.
And just as the camel
had almost reached the shadow of the tree
and the tiger
and the monkey
and the others were all getting ready —

the camel suddenly stopped,
and stretched her pretty neck
'way up in the sky.
And she opened her mouth —
oh, so wide, and
she let out an awful YAWN,
and said sweetly
in an ordinary sort of voice,

"I think I'll go back."

The tiger was so flabbergasted —
which means he was so surprised —
that, just when he should have —
HE DIDN'T POUNCE ON THE CAMEL.
AND THE MONKEY
DIDN'T DROP HIS COCOANUT.
THE SQUIRREL
DIDN'T BITE THE MONKEY'S TAIL.
AND THE BIRD
DIDN'T POUNCE
ON THE SQUIRREL'S HEAD.
And they didn't do all of these things
all in the same instant.

For just a tiny second no one said anything,
and not a sound was heard.

Then the little bird
burst into a peal of laughter
that pierced the forest.

The squirrel began to chatter
and the monkey began jumping up and down
with such glee
that all the creatures in the forest
woke up crying,
"What happened? What happened?"

But you *know* what happened.
Nothing happened.
The beautiful camel just turned around
and walked back the same way she had come.
The tiger *slinked* away
into the deep dark forest.
And the sun shone like brass in the sky.